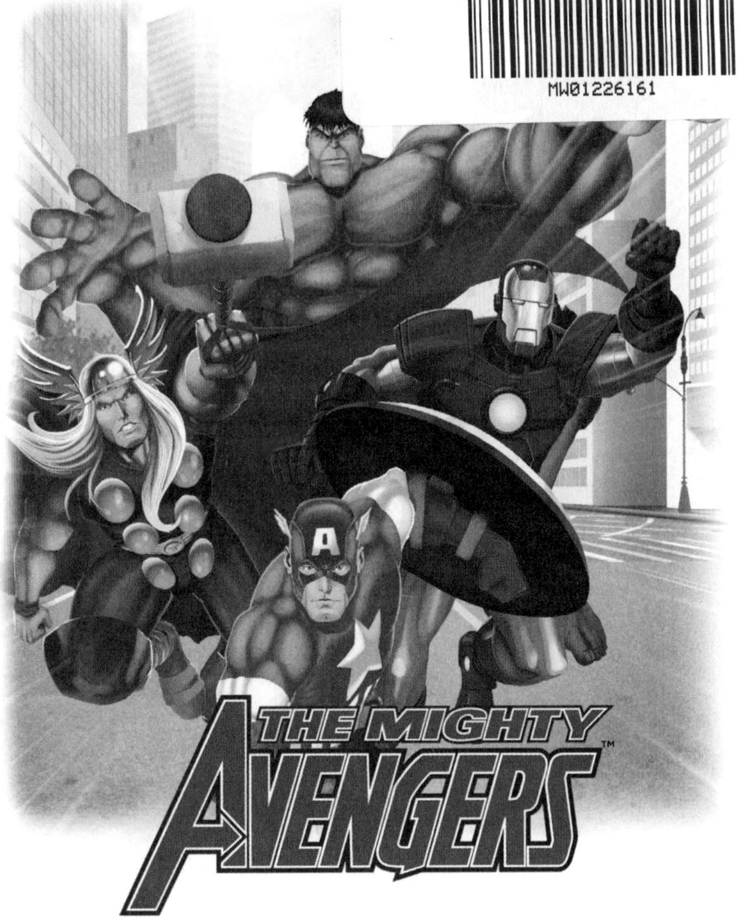
THE MIGHTY
AVENGERS™

Based on the Marvel comic book series The Avengers
Adapted by Billy Wrecks
Illustrated by Patrick Spaziante

A GOLDEN BOOK • NEW YORK

 Published in the United States by Golden Books, an imprint of Random House Children's Books, a division of Penguin Random House LLC, 1745 Broadway, New York, NY 10019, and in Canada by Penguin Random House Canada Limited, Toronto. Golden Books, A Golden Book, A Little Golden Book, the G colophon, and the distinctive gold spine are registered trademarks of Penguin Random House LLC.
rhcbooks.com

ISBN 978-0-307-93109-2 (trade) — ISBN 978-0-399-55922-8 (ebook)

Printed in the United States of America

25 24 23 22 21 20

When Earth is in great danger, the world's mightiest super heroes assemble. Together they are known as . . .

The Avengers!

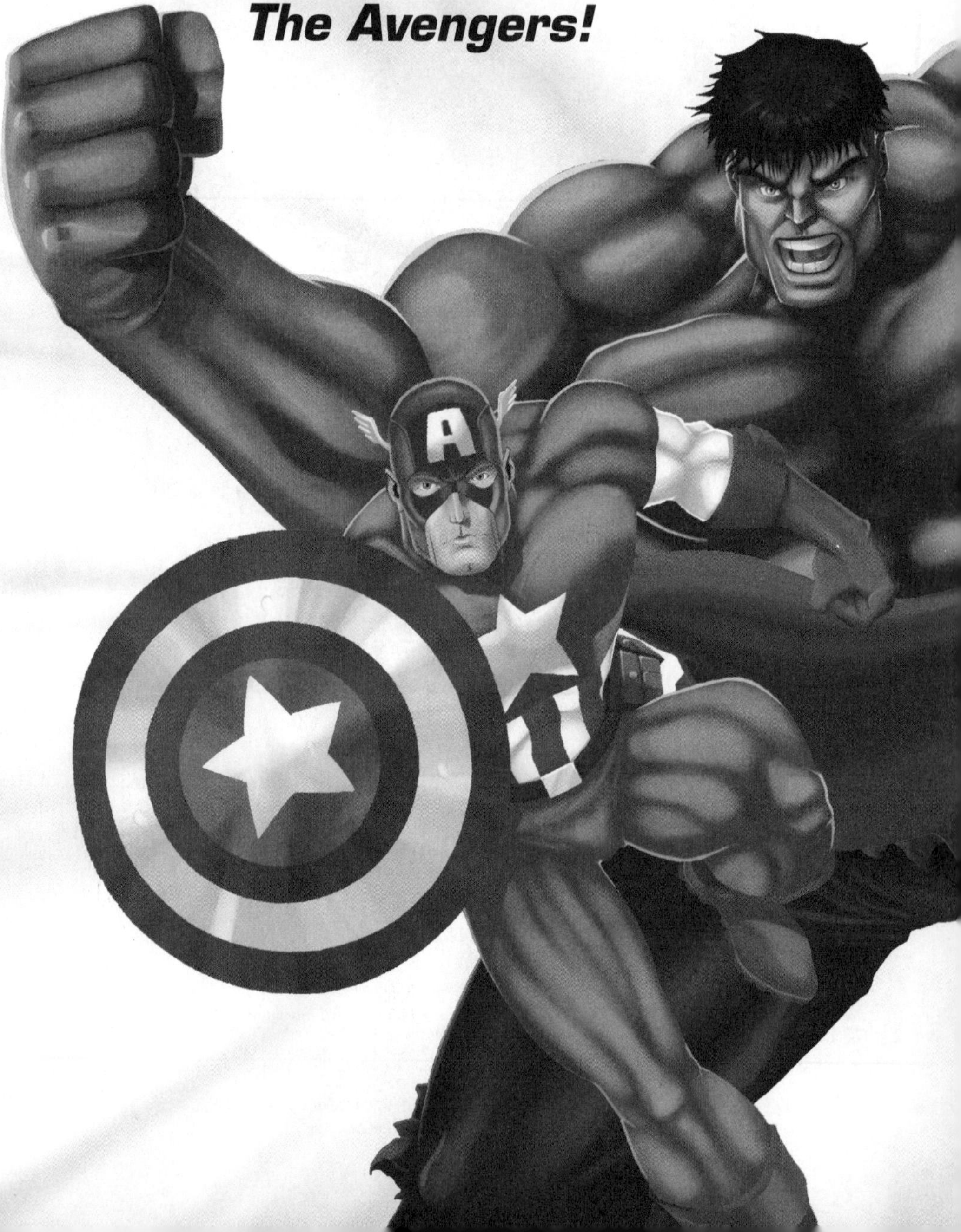

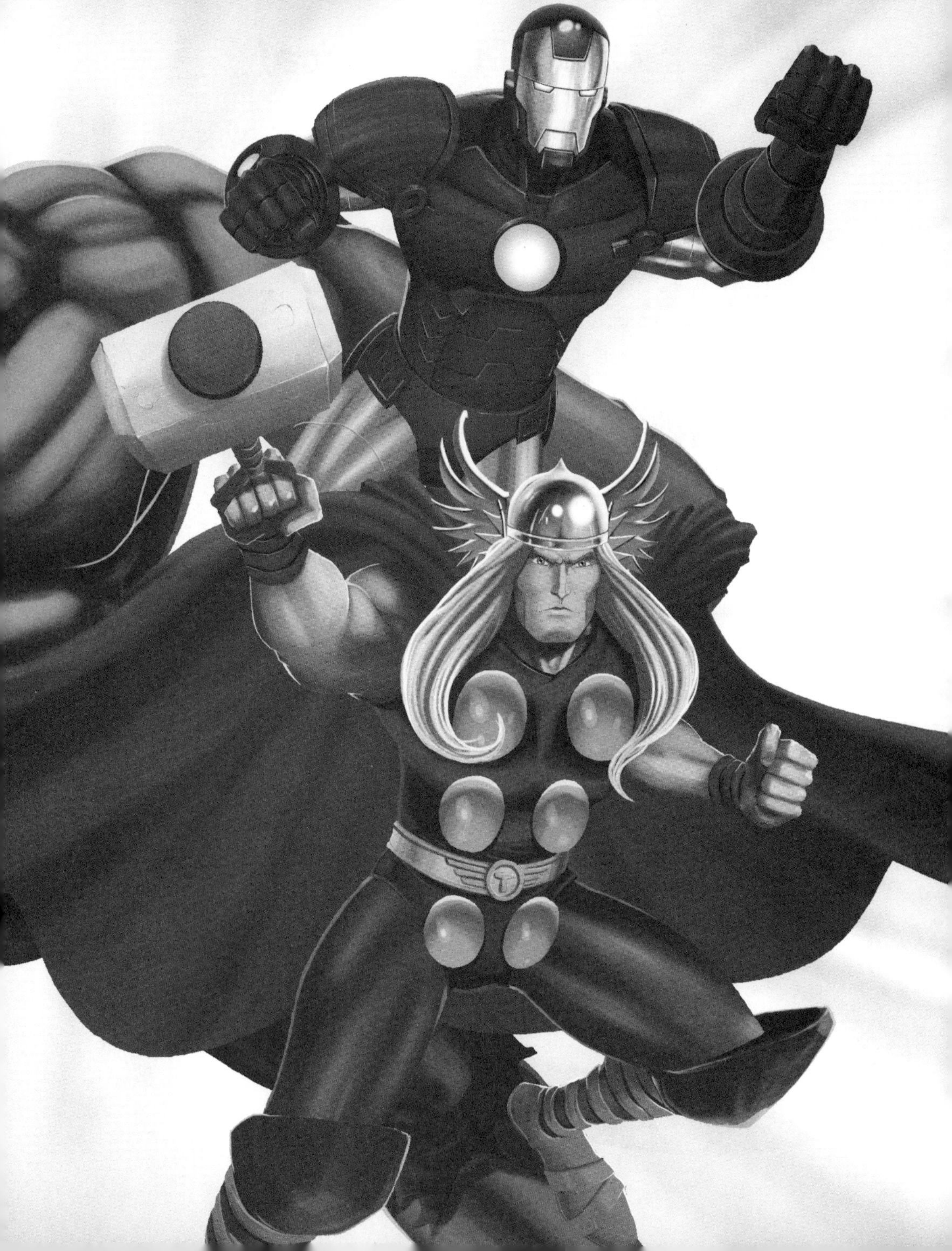

Captain America!

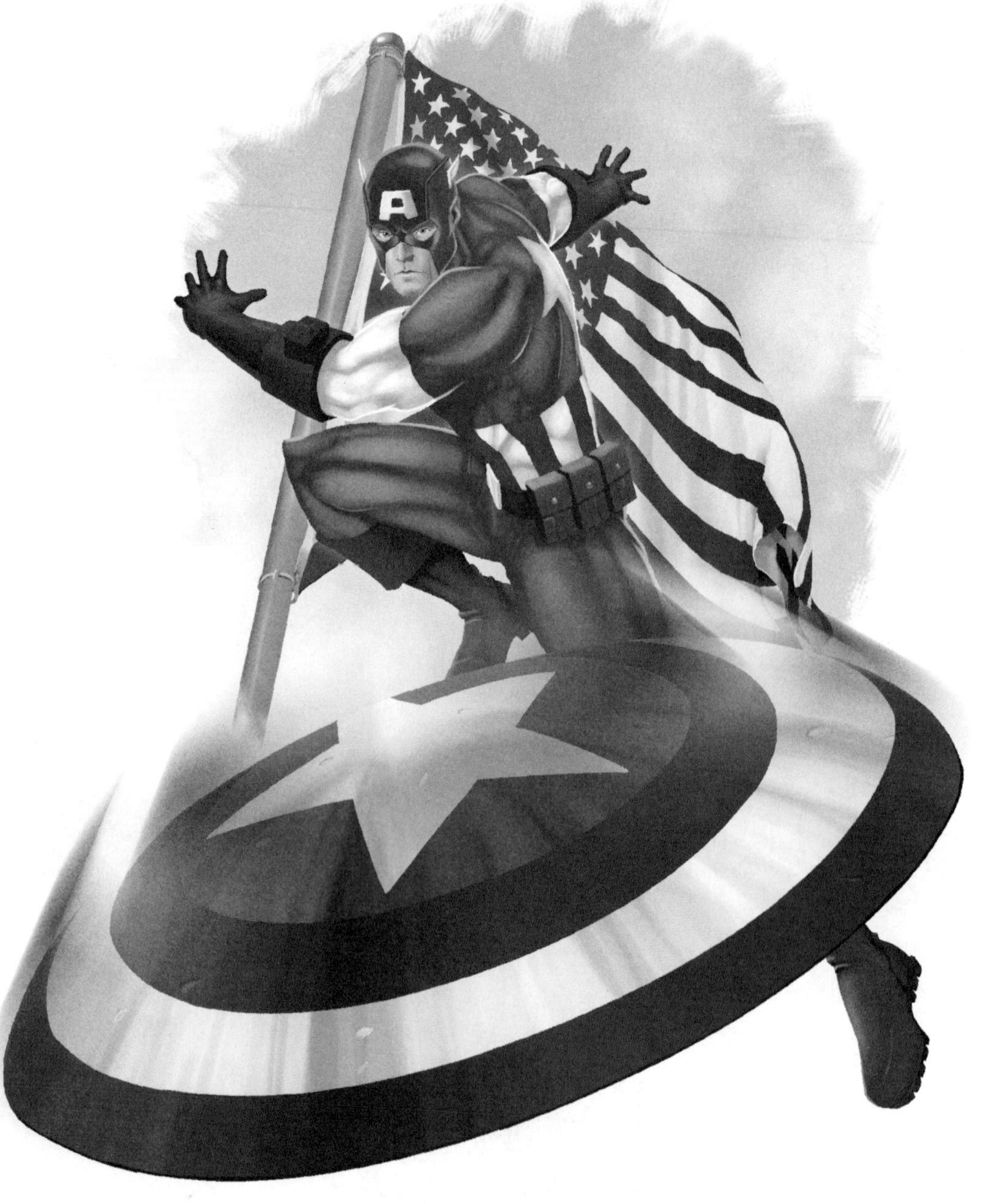

A

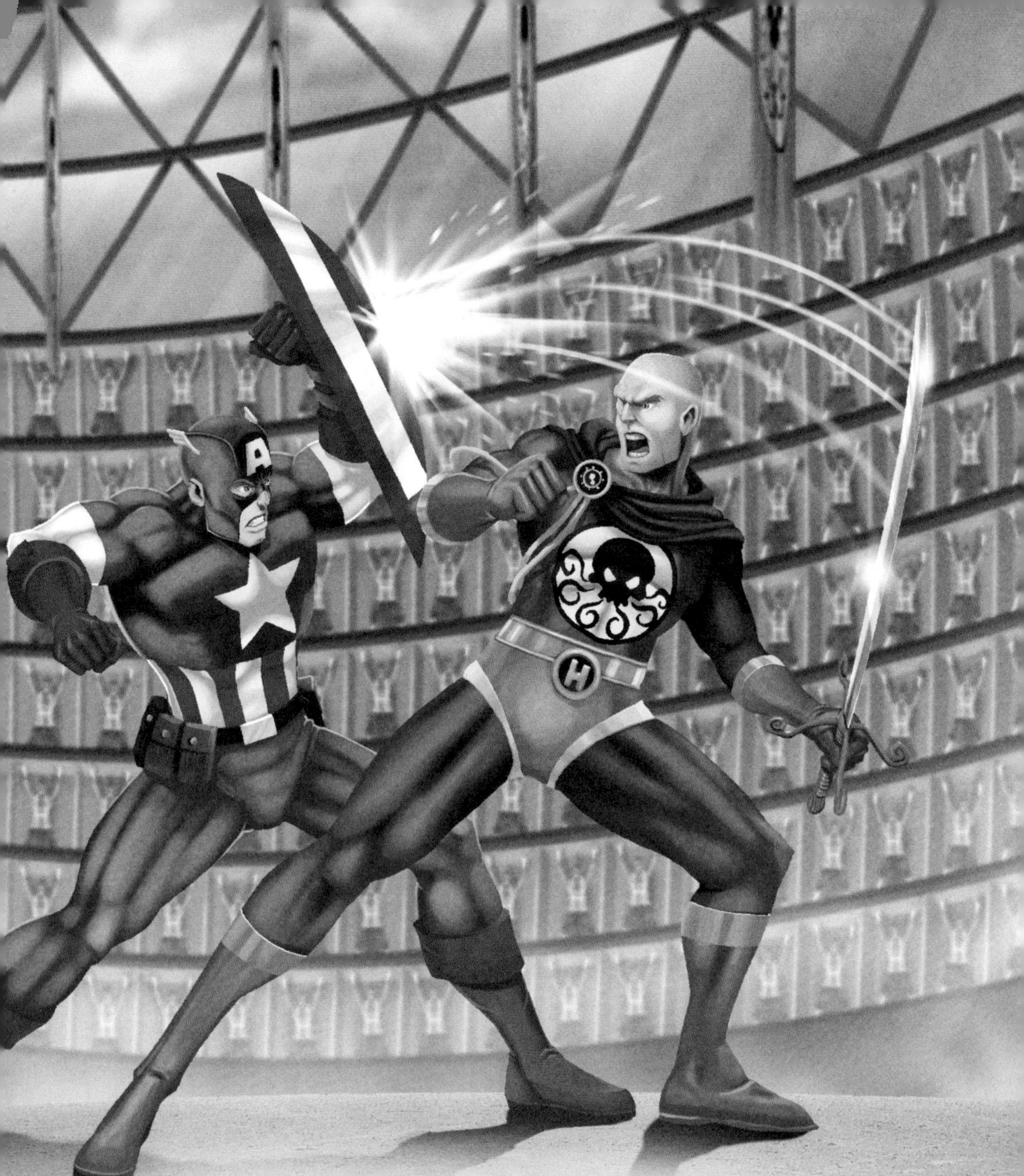

Captain America has the strength and speed of a great athlete. With his unbreakable shield, Captain America leads the Avengers in their never-ending fight to defend truth, justice, and freedom.

Iron Man!

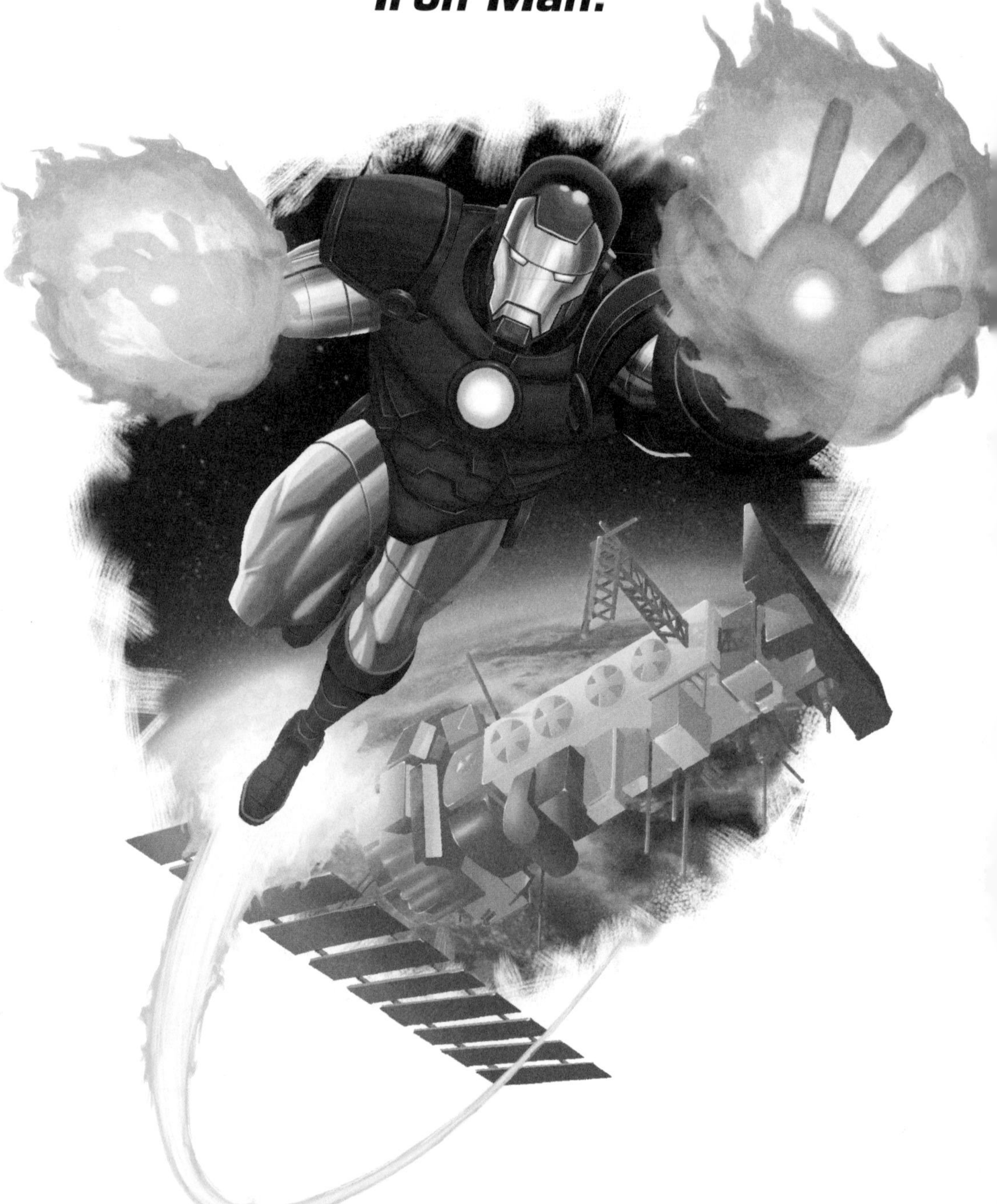

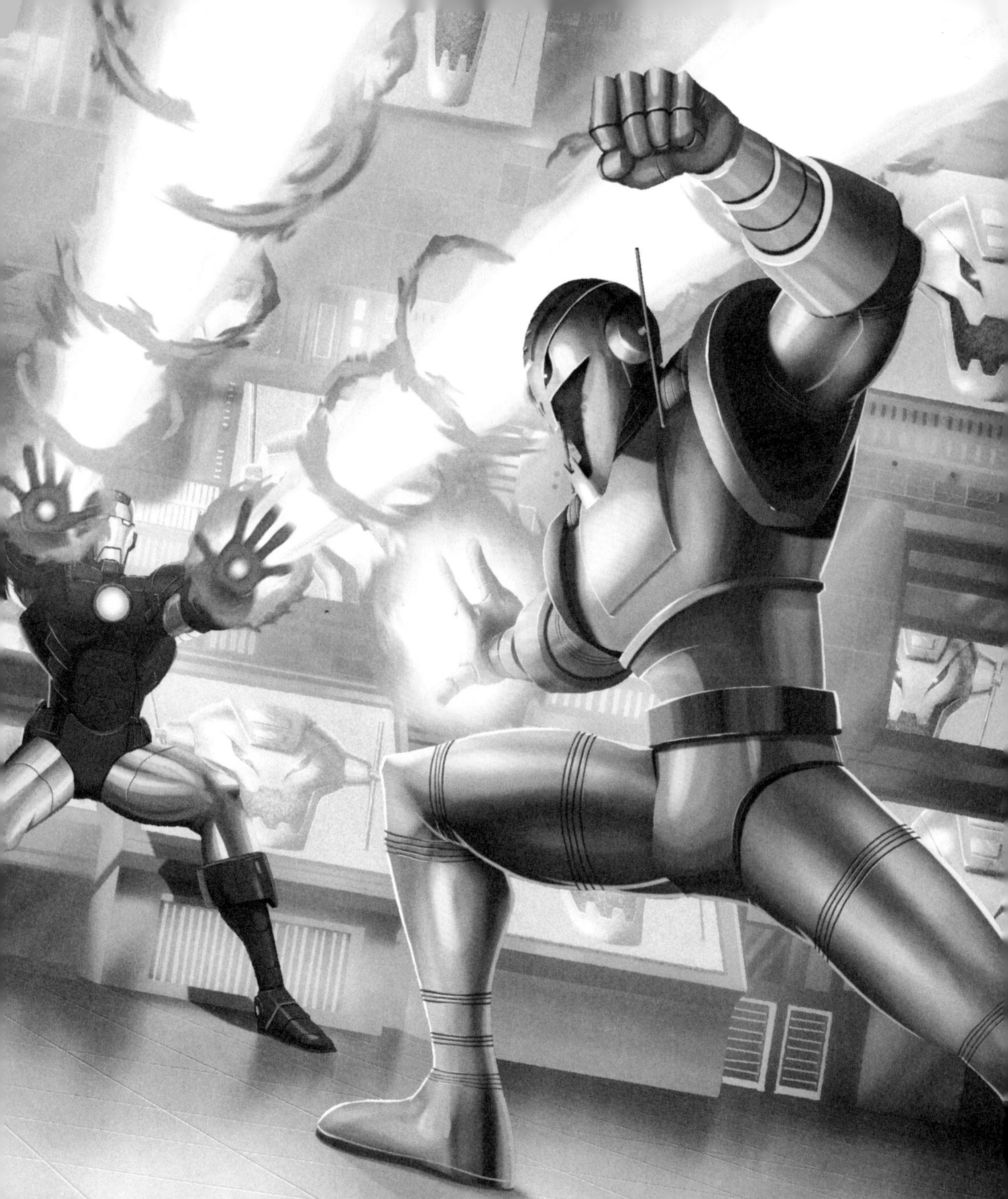

Iron Man wears armor that allows him to fly and fire powerful repulsor rays! Iron Man keeps the Avengers one step ahead of the super criminals who use advanced technology for their far-reaching plots.

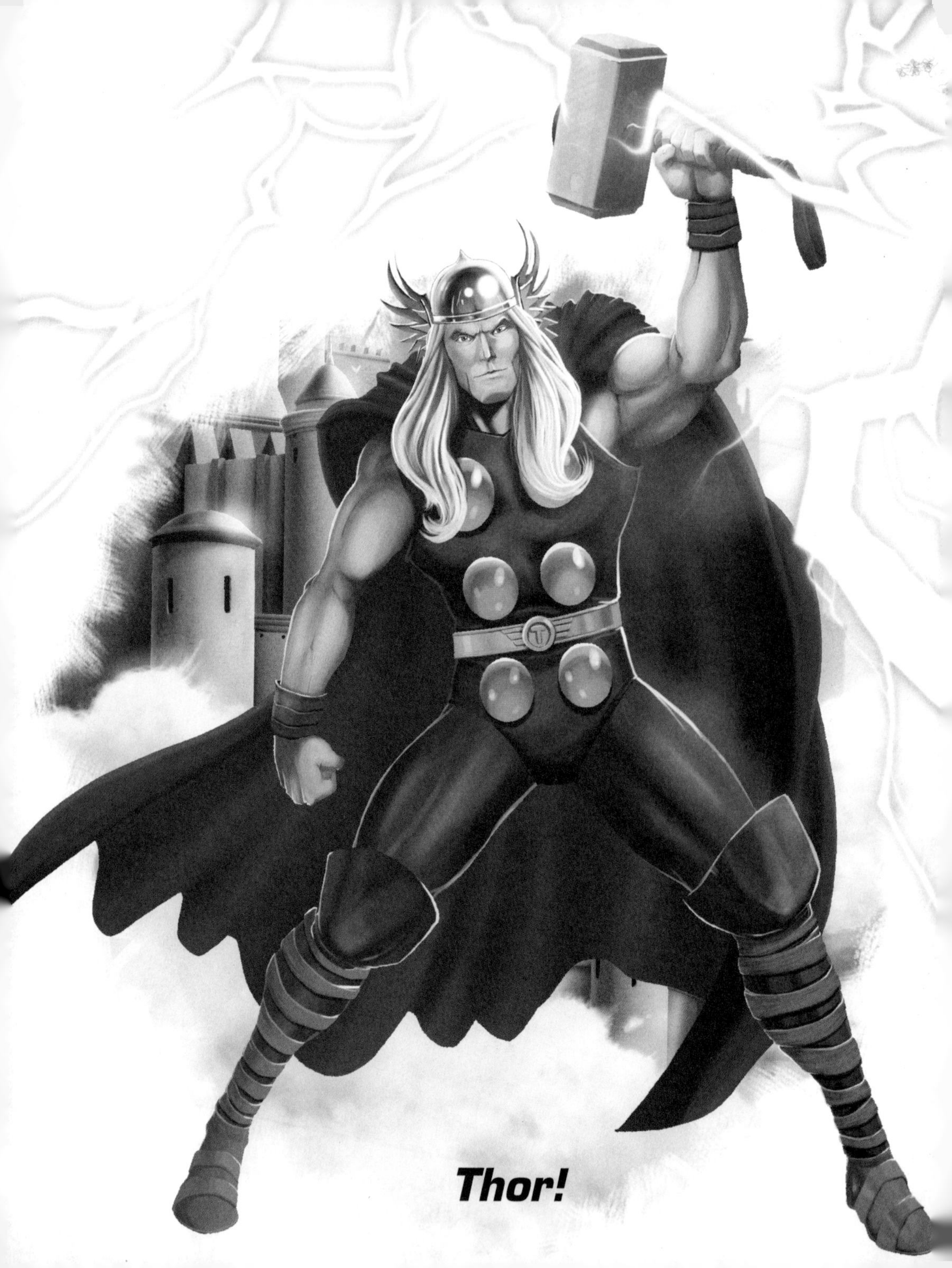

Thor!

Thor can control wind, rain, and lightning! When he spins his magical hammer, Thor can fly through the air at amazing speeds.

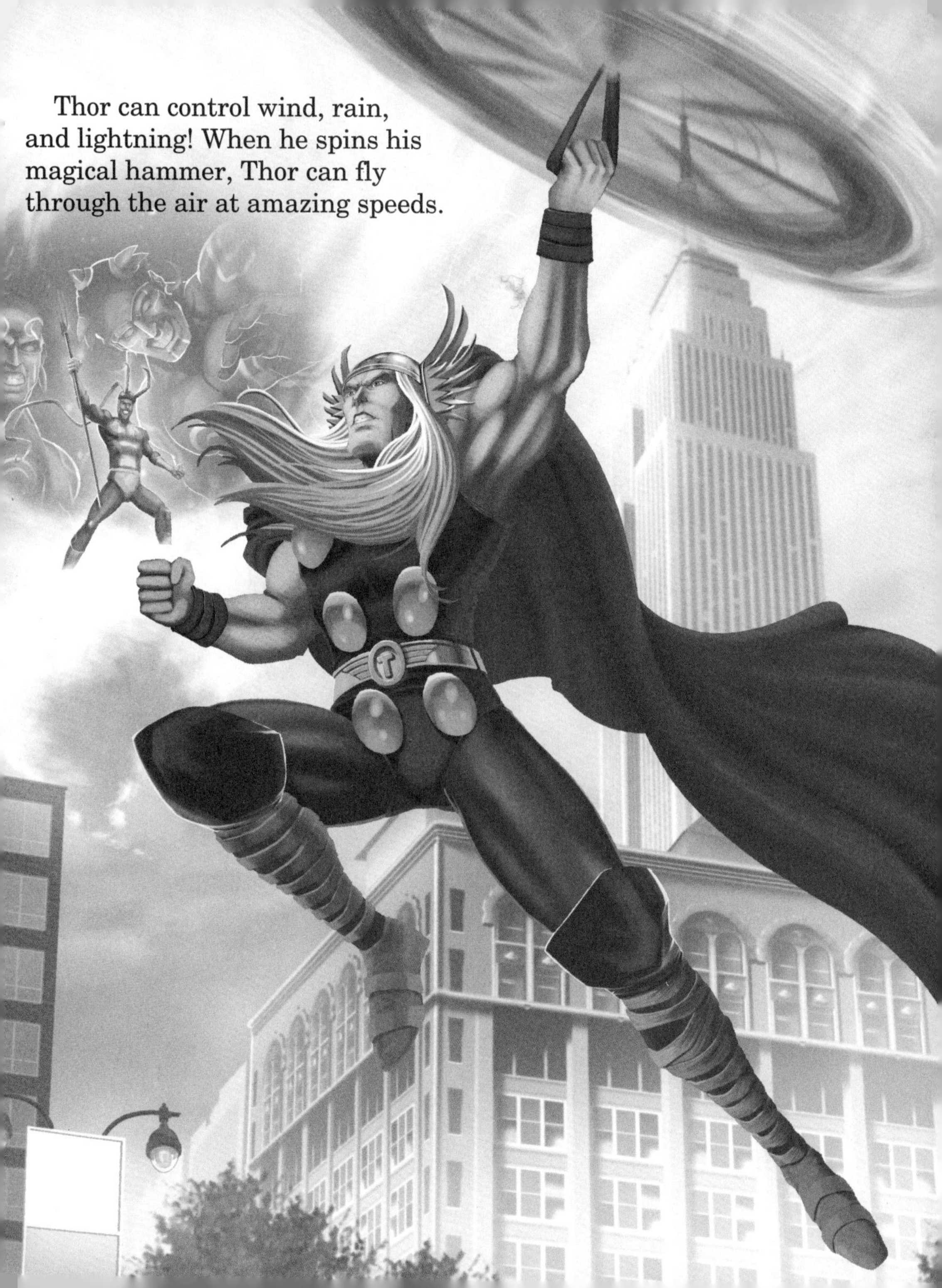

Hulk!

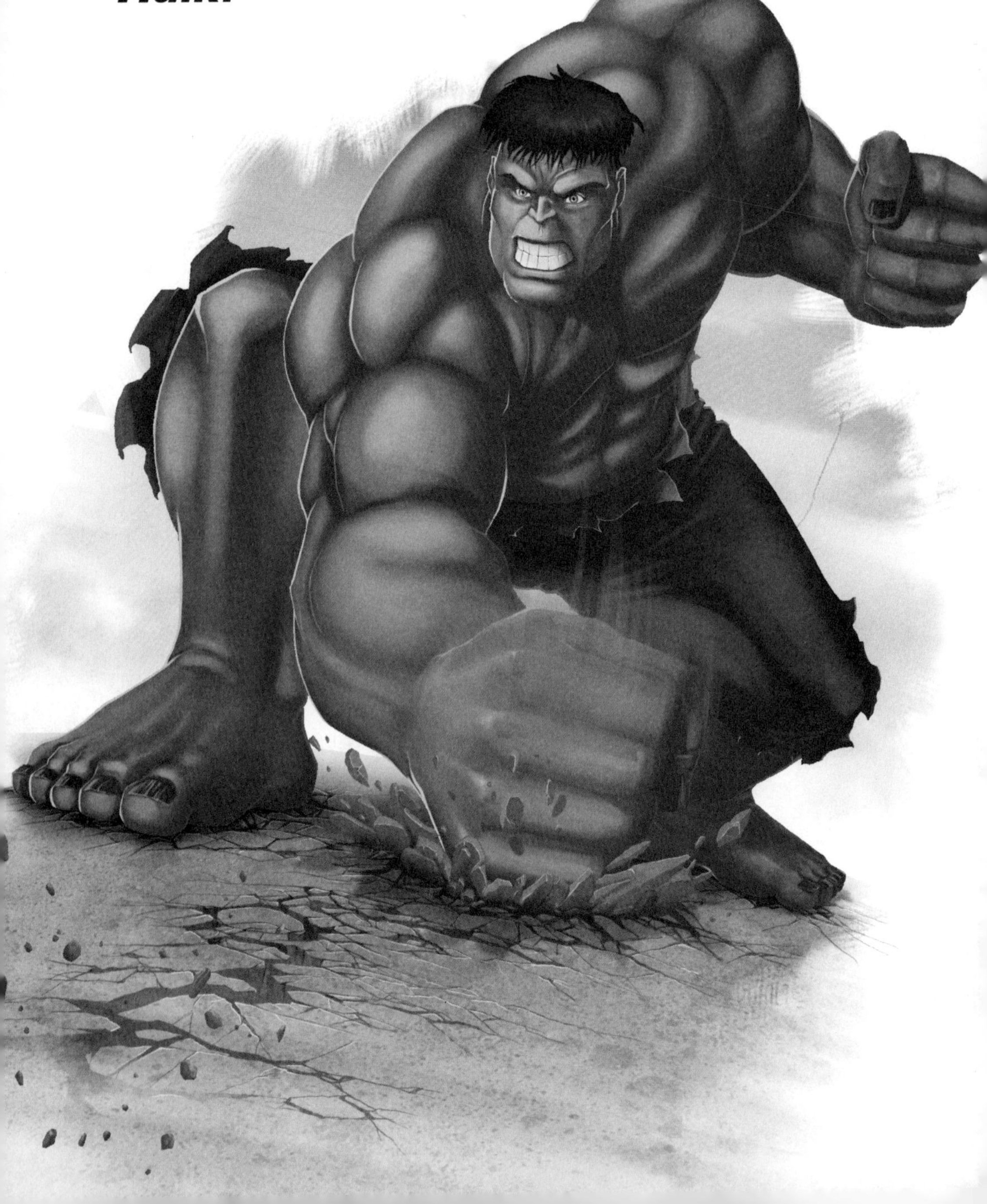

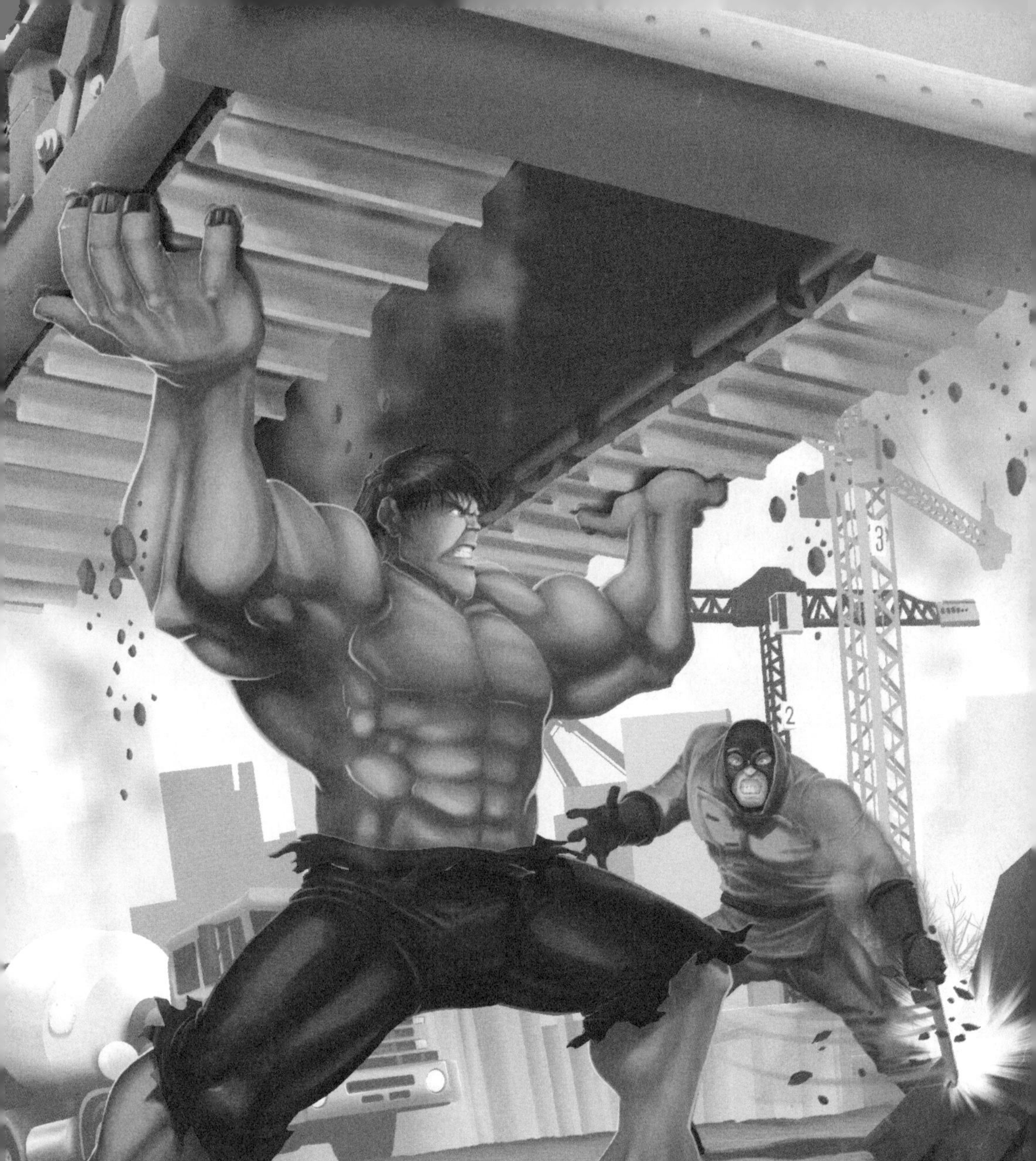

Hulk is the strongest hero there is! When the Avengers must face one of their toughest enemies, Hulk is the green-skinned giant for the job.

The criminal organization called **HYDRA** wants to take over the world! But they will never succeed, because the Avengers will always stand in their way.

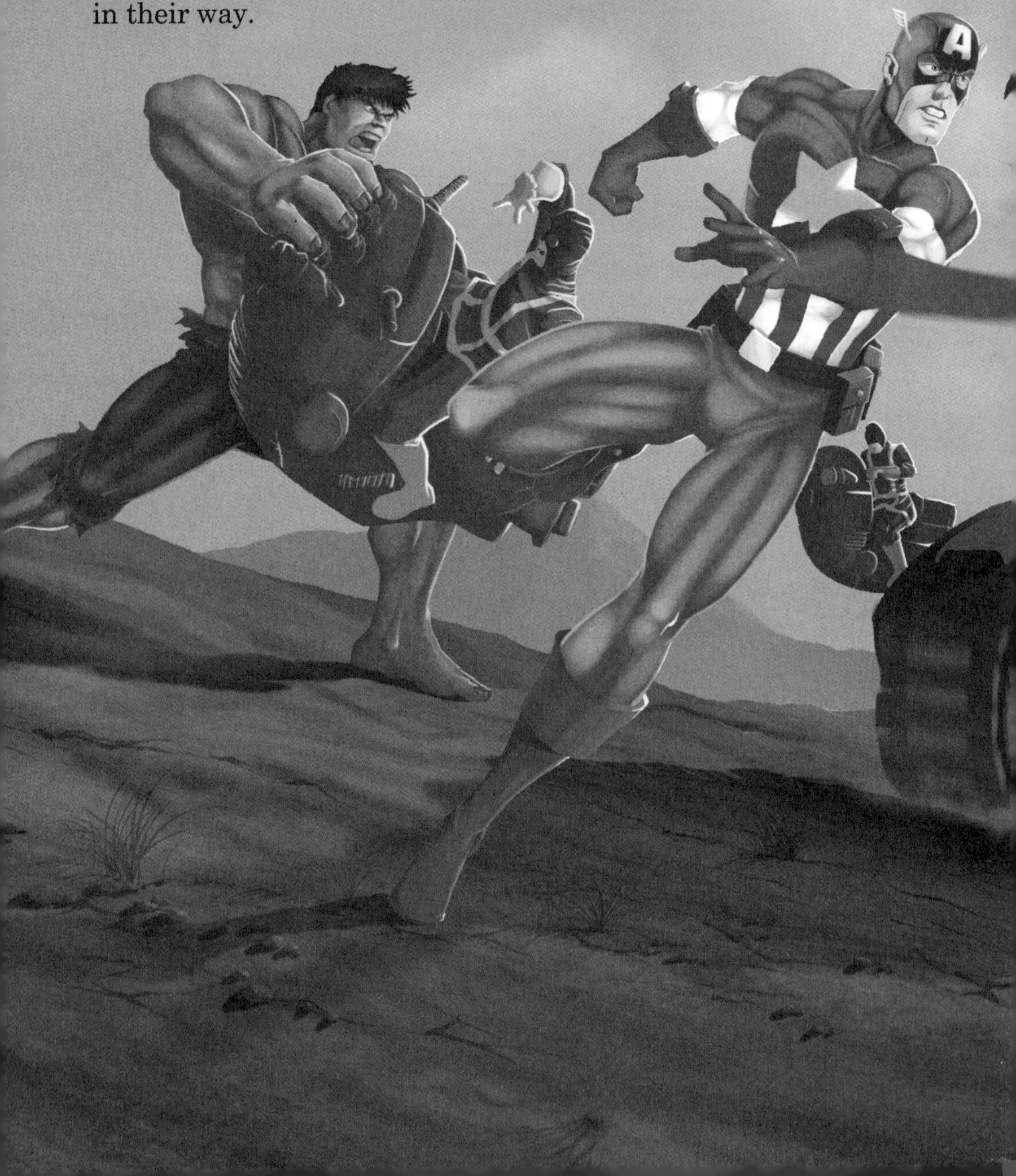

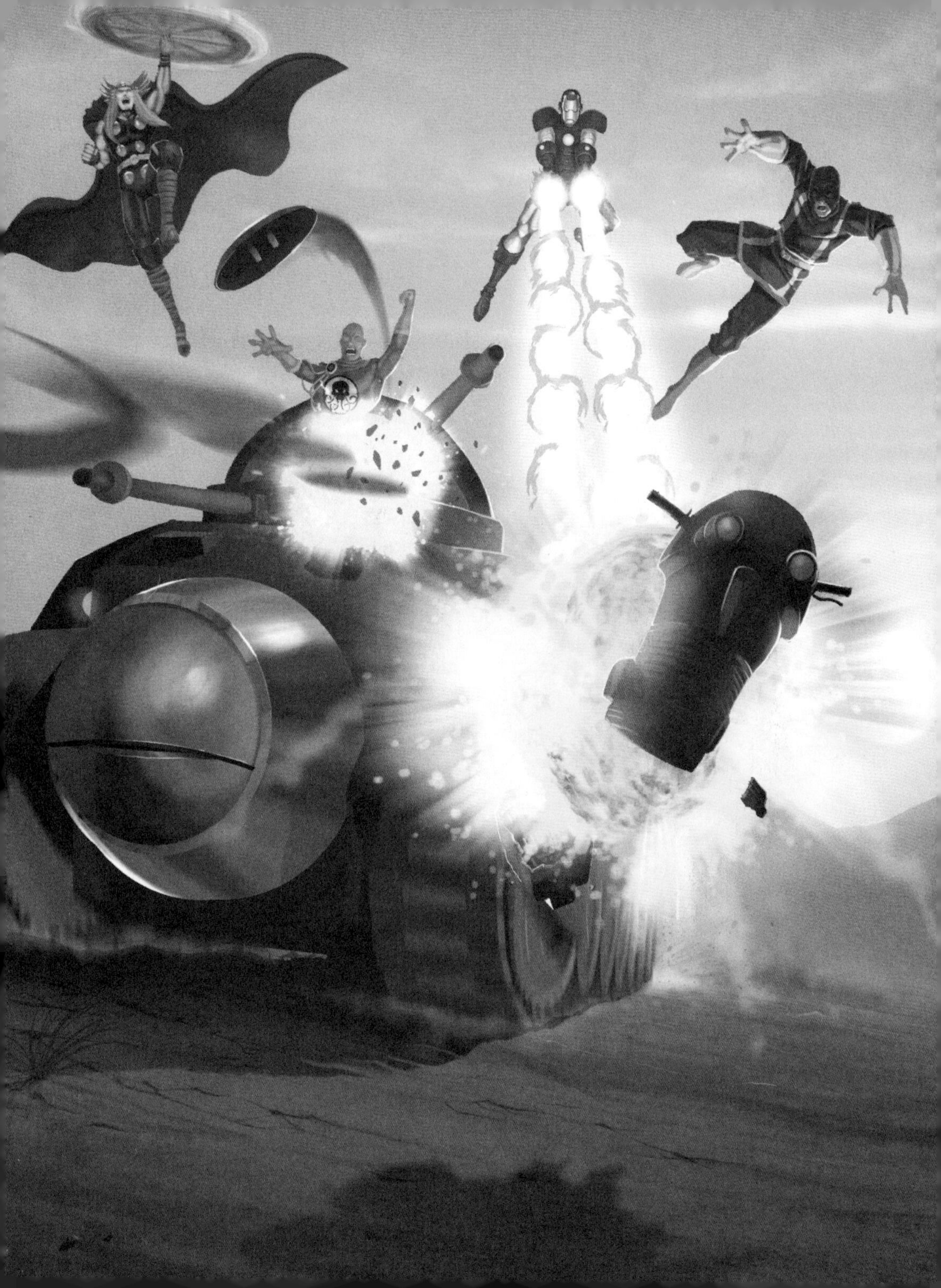

The ***Wrecker*** and the Wrecking Crew are superstrong bullies who think they can take whatever they want, whenever they want it! Luckily, the Avengers have the courage to take them on—any time and any place!

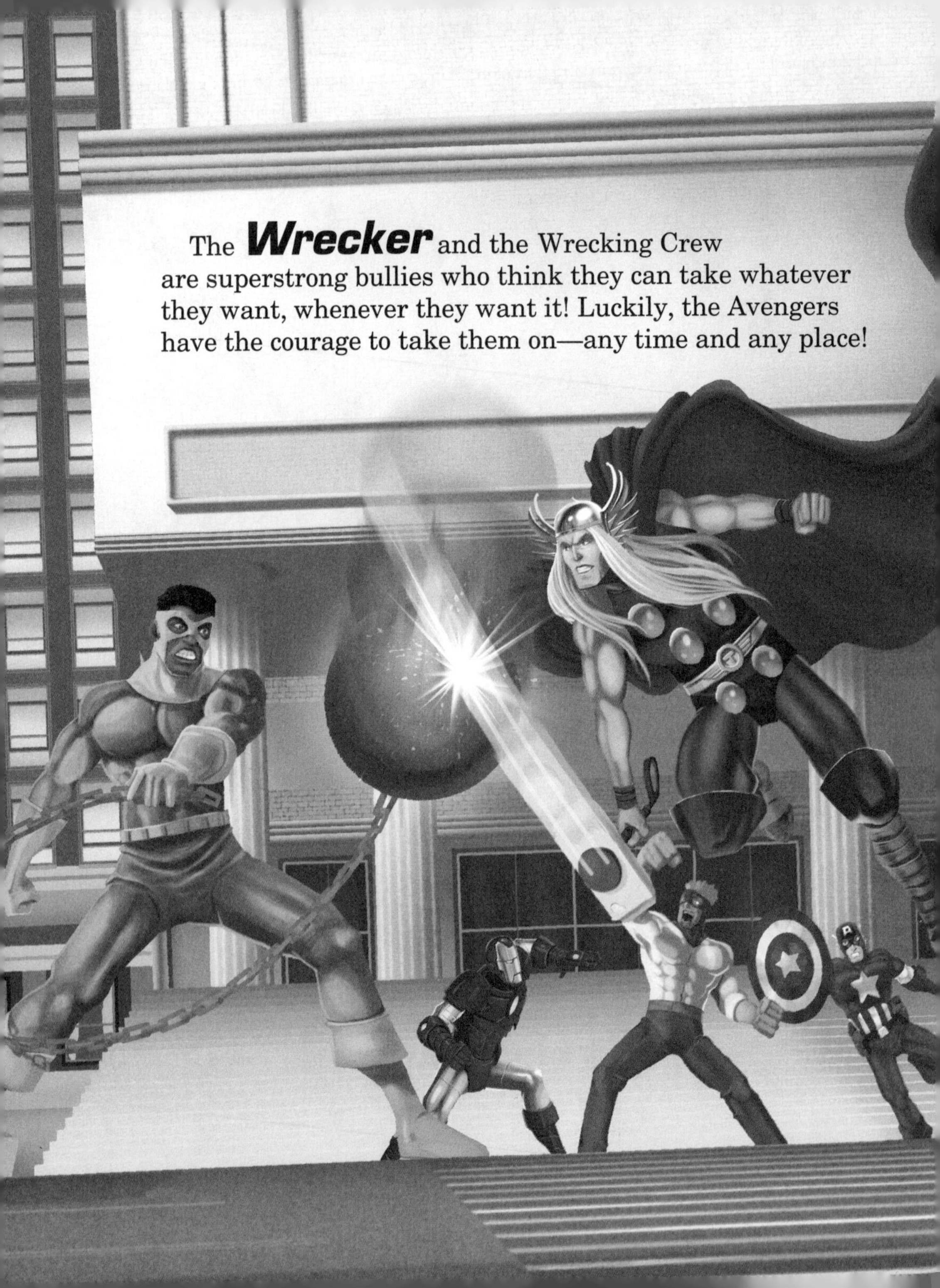

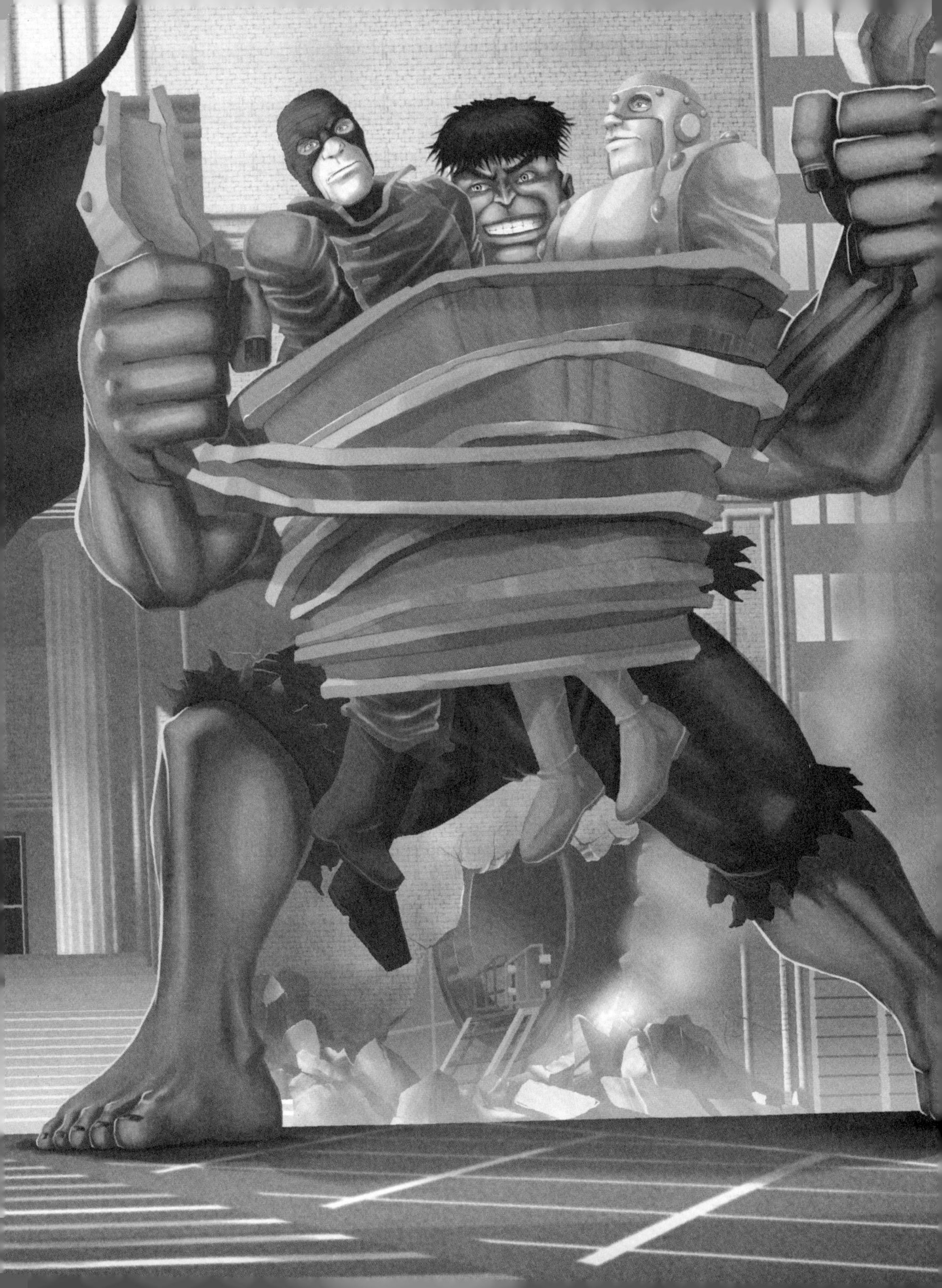

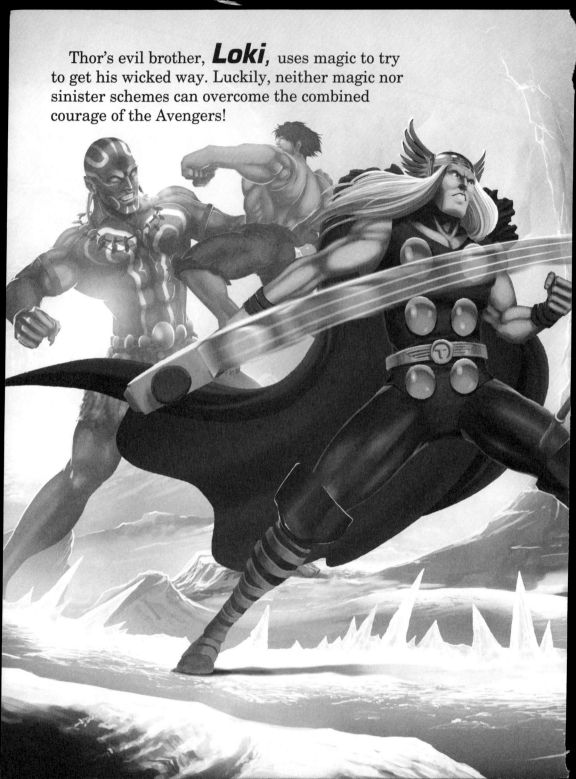

Thor's evil brother, **Loki,** uses magic to try
to get his wicked way. Luckily, neither magic nor
sinister schemes can overcome the combined
courage of the Avengers!

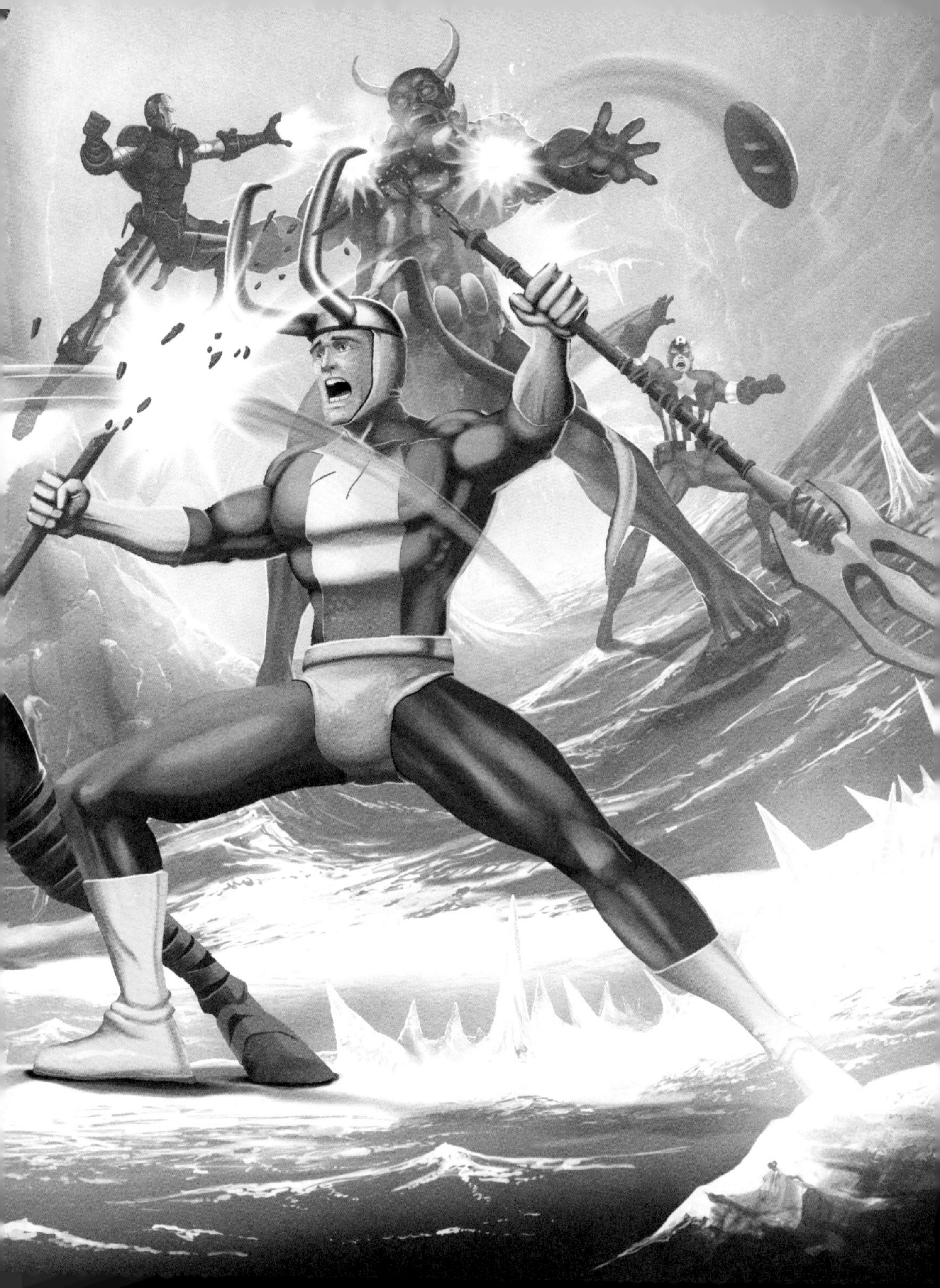

Ultron is an indestructible robot determined to rule the universe! But super science and advanced technology are no match for the might of the Avengers when they use teamwork to face this powerful foe.

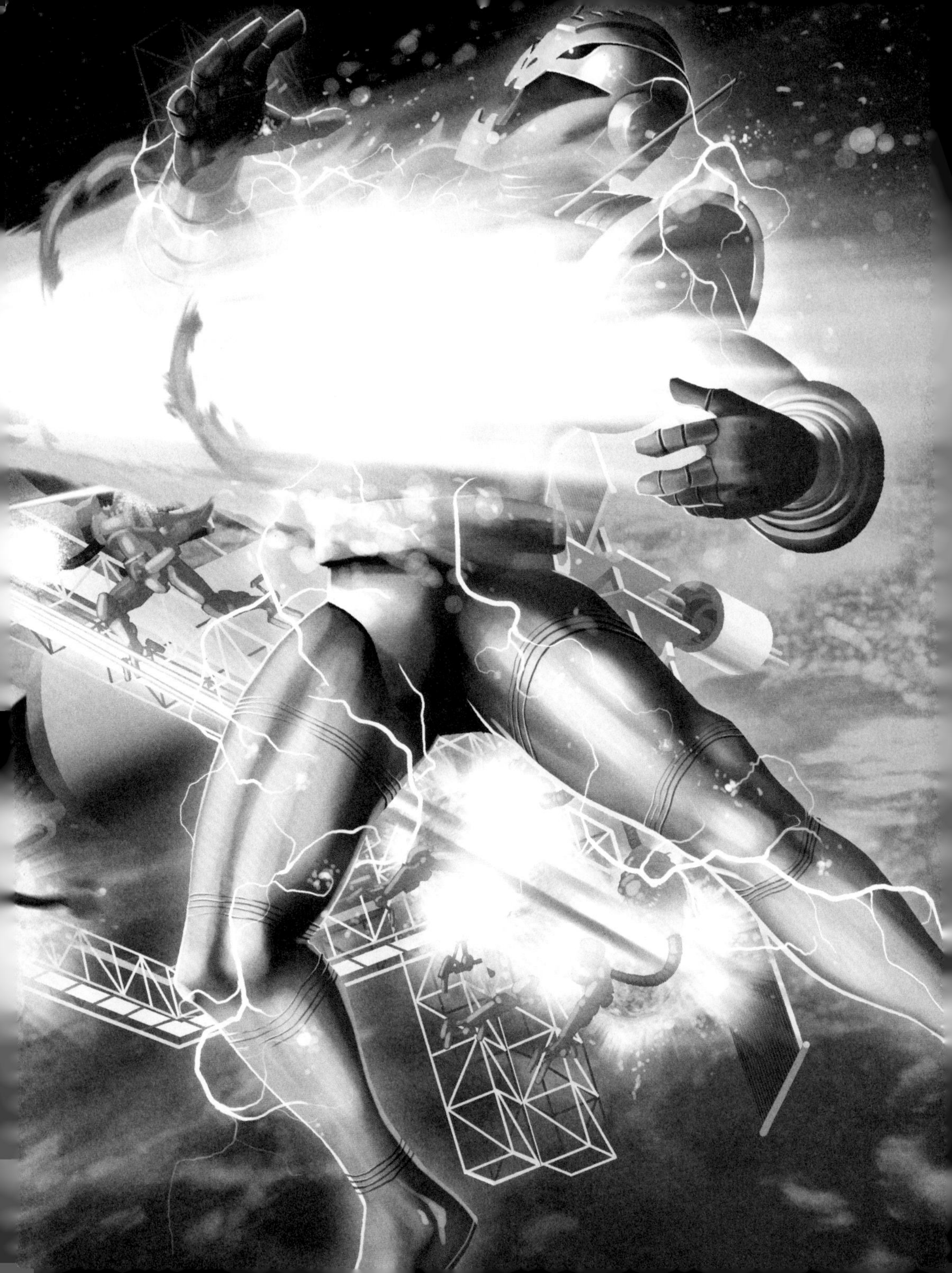

After stopping the bad guys, the Avengers take them to a high-tech prison called the ***Vault***. Locked away, the villains can do no more harm—but they're always looking for a way to escape!

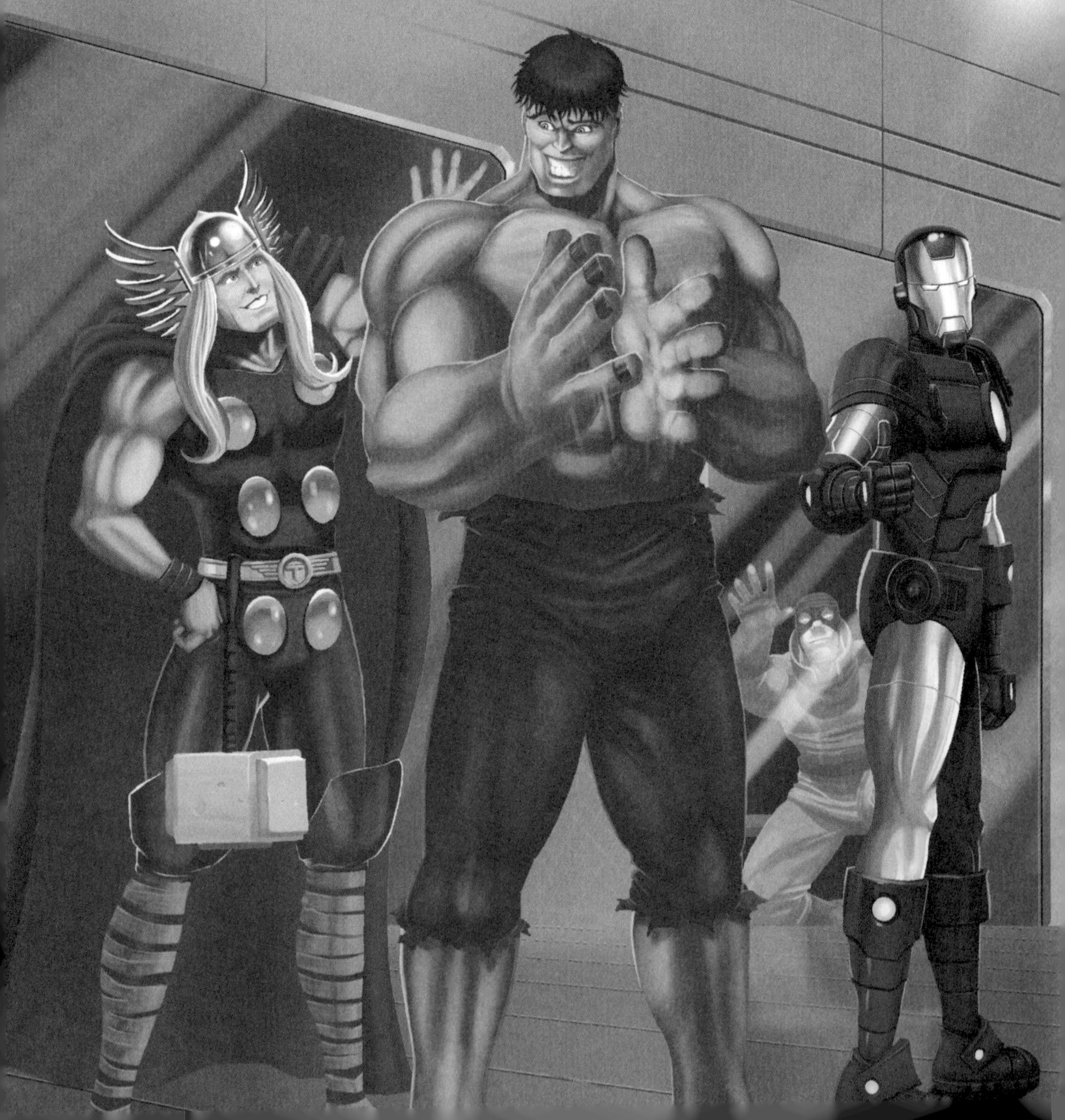

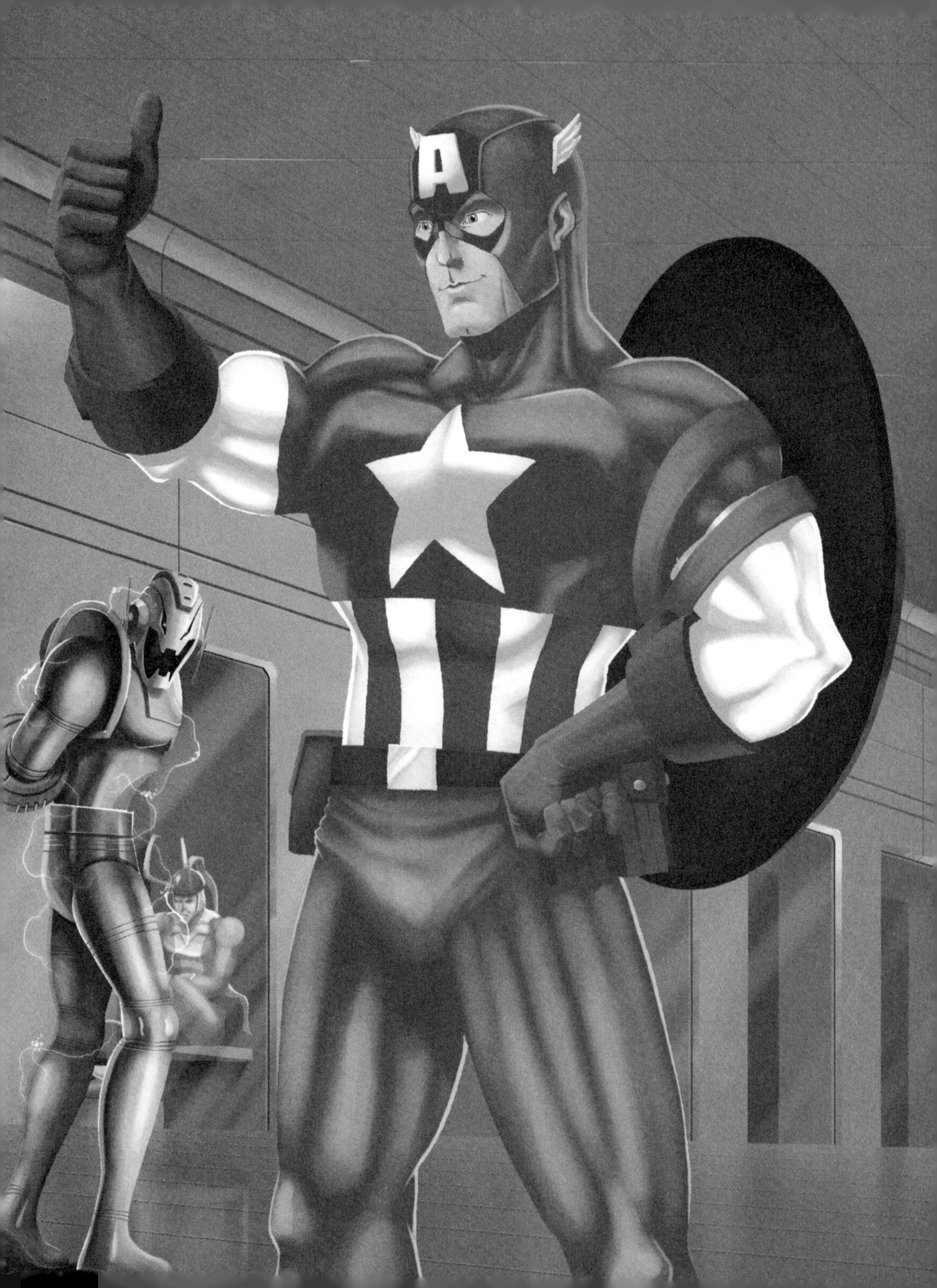

Captain America, Iron Man, Thor, and Hulk are amazing heroes on their own. But as the Avengers, their combined super powers are an unstoppable force for good!

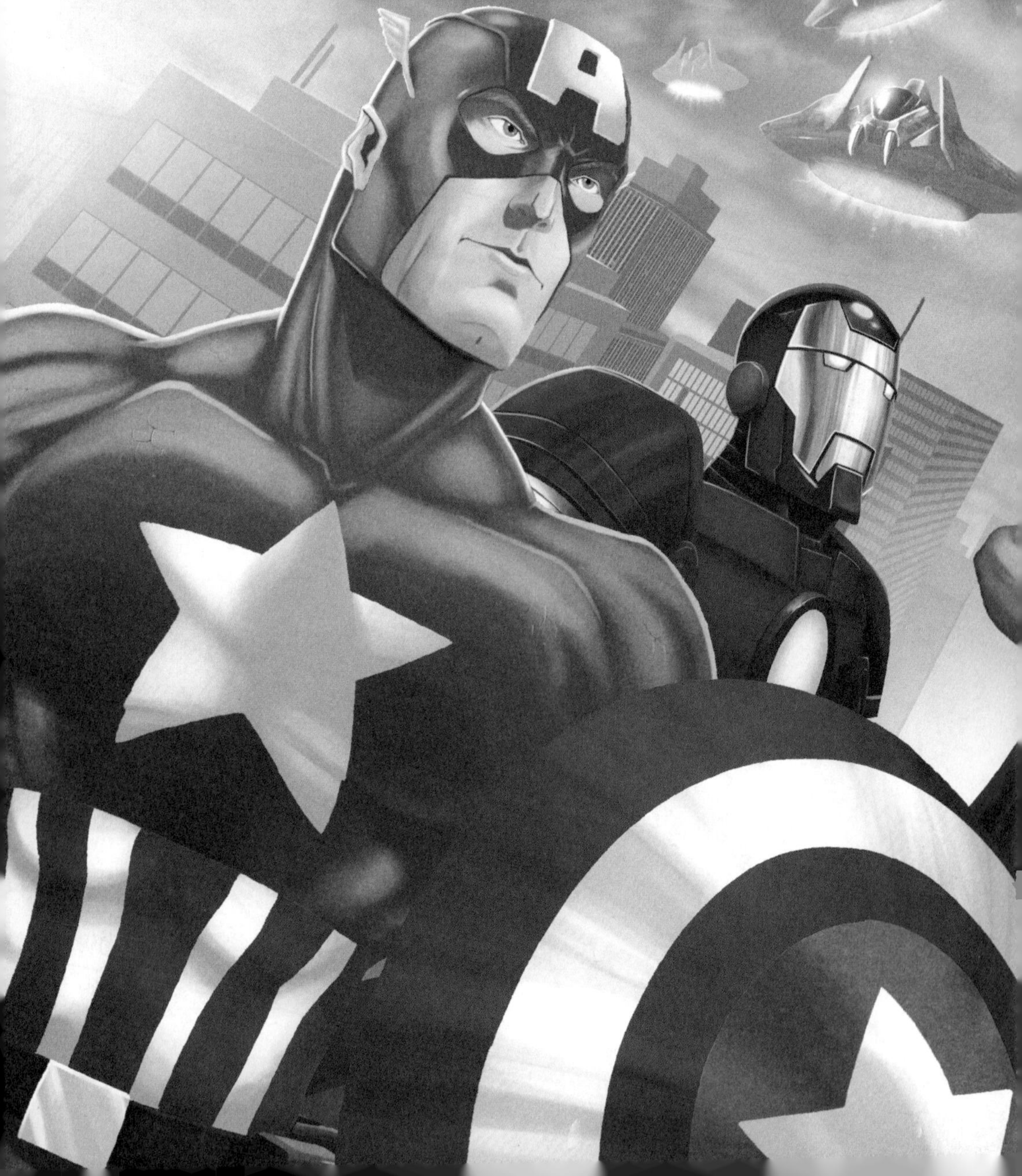

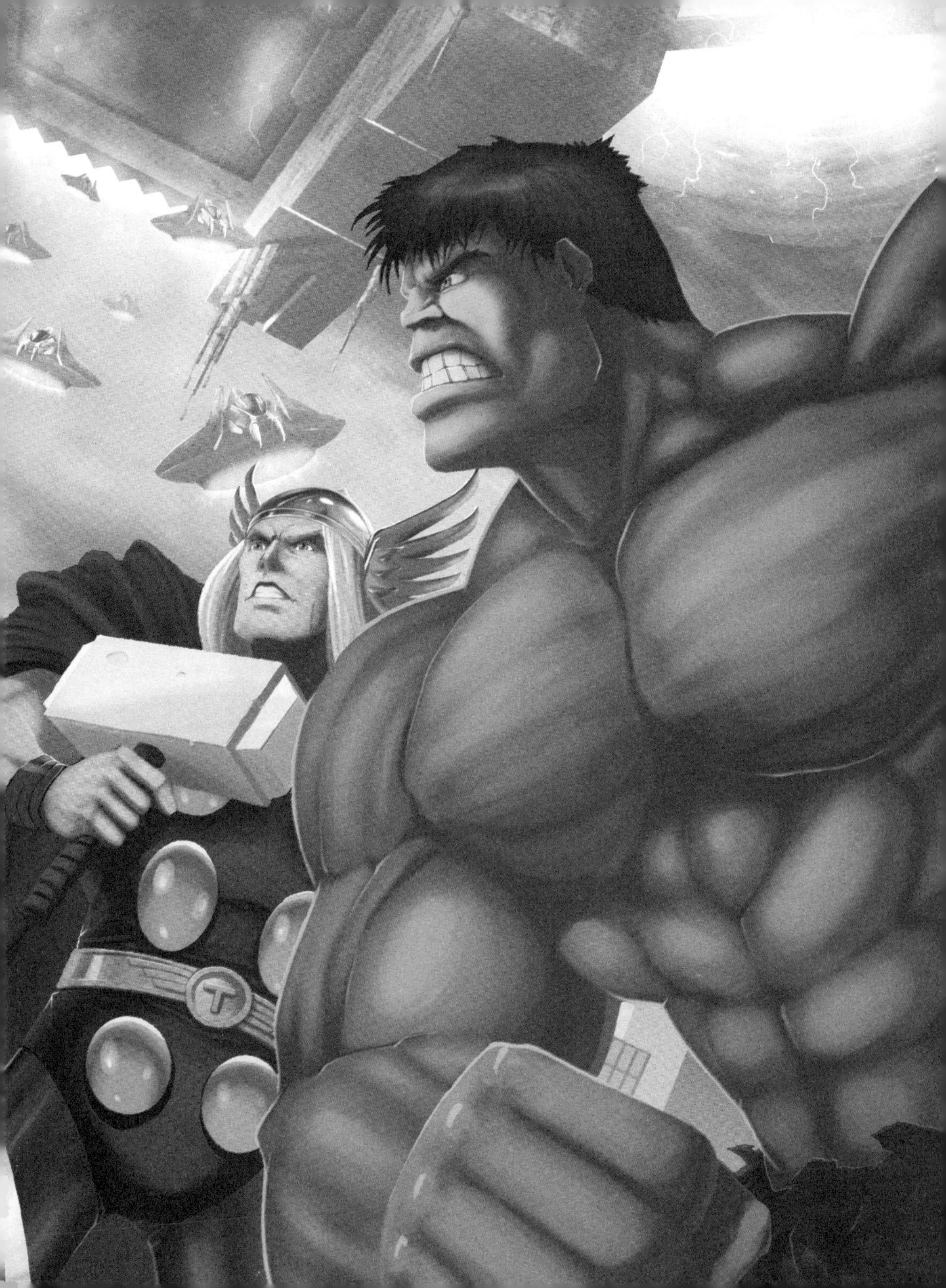

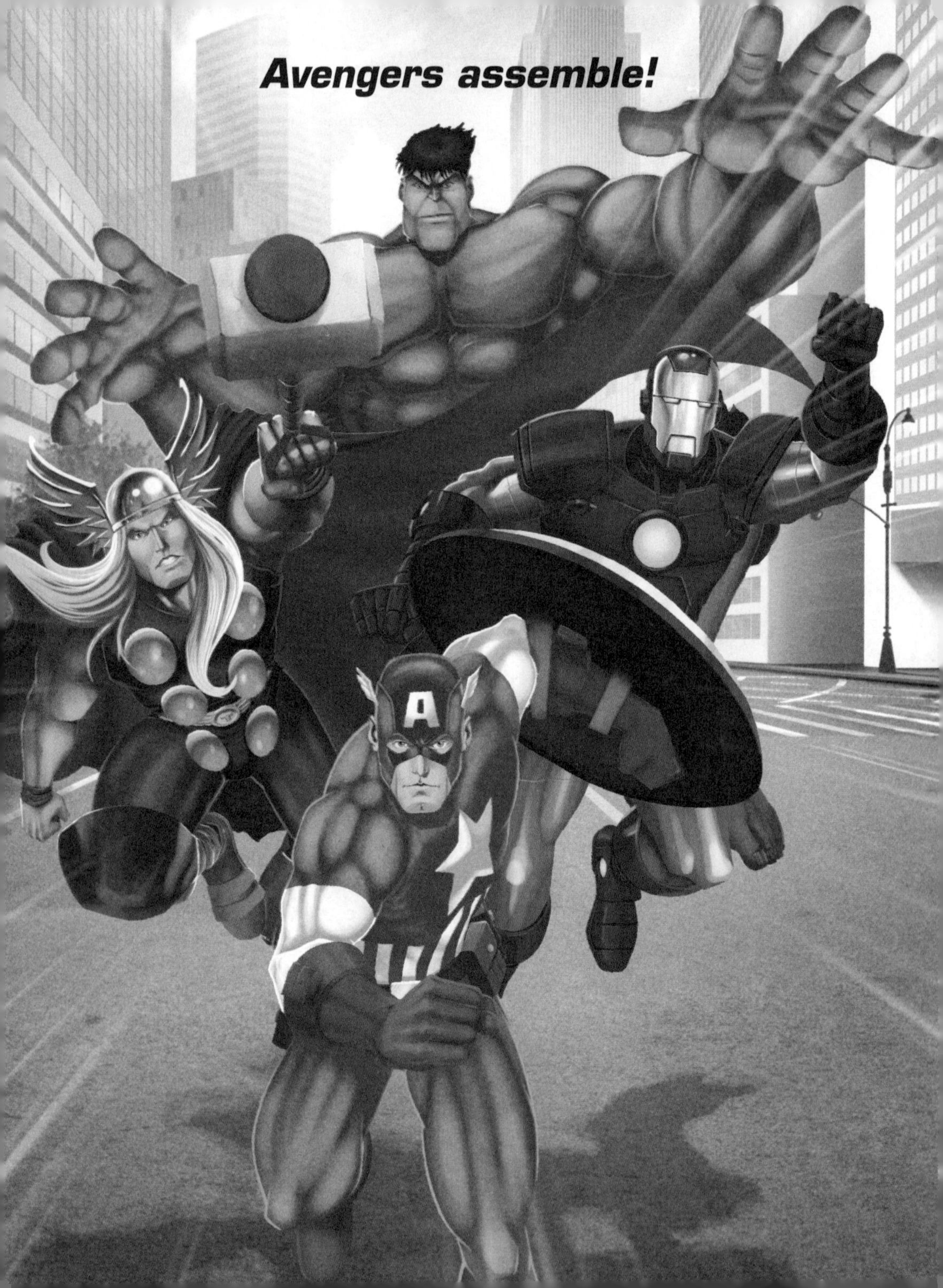
Avengers assemble!